SO YOU'VE GONE AND DONE A BREXIT

GOVERNMENTAL ADVICE FOR SURVIVING FOOD SHORTAGES MAKING YOUR OWN MEDICINE AND SACRIFICING LOVED ONES.

(A HappyToast parody)

Disclaimer

This is written as a bit of nonsense, don't bother picking the grammar apart because I really don't care and life and Brexit are going to be hard enough without getting upset about why I did or didn't place a comma where I did.This is a parody, a work of dark humour. No offence intended. I'm just trying to laugh at the madness, otherwise the horror befalling the people that didn't vote for Brexit is too much. If you class yourself as a gammon or believe this to be in any way a serious instruction manual and end up eating your own children that's your own fault. No science or research was involved in the making of this book.

Patreon.com/HappyToast

@IamHappyToast

HappyToastArts

Layout and formatting - Jelzoo.com

First (and last) edition

ISBN: 9781798900260

For Mrs Toast, Captain Howdy
and everyone who voted Remain

May we live long enough
to laugh about this.

READ THIS BOOKLET WITH CARE.

YOUR LIFE AND THE LIVES OF YOUR FAMILY MAY DEPEND ON IT.

DO AS IT ADVISES.

KEEP IT SAFELY AT HAND.

CONTENTS

PREFACE

If the country were ever stupid enough to vote to leave the European Union, perhaps having been convinced to do so following a long campaign of misinformation and lies in the national press or because they saw a nice slogan on a big red bus, then a copy of this booklet would be distributed to every household. This would form part of a public information campaign which may include announcements on television and radio, short art-house films in cinemas, irritating pop-up ads in computer games, disguised as Facebook friend requests and via angry people stood on street corners shouting in to loud-hailers or even directly through your letter box.

The booklet has been designed for general distribution in that event at a reasonable price from very specific retailers.

If the United Kingdom is placed under attack from Brexit we do not know exactly how severe the assault will be. Such disastrous consequences are impossible to fully predict, which is why we are quite certain such an event would never happen. No one could be that stupid. If however insanity reigns, those of us living in the rural areas might be exposed to as great a risk as those in the towns and cities. No part of the United Kingdom can be considered safe from the direct effects of Brexit.

The dangers which you and your family will face in this situation can be reduced if you do as this booklet describes.

This book is a work of fiction and shouldn't be taken seriously.

INTRODUCTION

What is Brexit?

Brexit is a non-binding, corrupt vote pushed through by the Prime Minister initially as an attempt to stabilize the Conservative Party but which became an exercise in Disaster Capitalism. Stripping the entire country of its value before buying it all up cheap and then selling it back to the public at inflated prices.

How did it happen?

After years of propaganda in the tabloid press convincing the public that the EU were evil and controlling the shape of bananas, some MPs saw the opportunity to use this misinformation as a way of grabbing power. With additional lies plastered on buses and pointing a finger of blame at innocent people fleeing war, the public were sufficiently manipulated in to voting for the unthinkable - that is, they weren't thinking when they voted. Also the government provided an incredibly vague in/out option which as you can probably tell by now, was a fucking ridiculous over-simplification of the whole issue.

Why wasn't it stopped?

That's a really good question.

What now?

It is important not to panic, unless panicking gives you an edge, in which case do that. Get out and gather supplies as soon as possible.

Time is running out and vital resources will be getting scarce. It's probably like Mad Max out there already so before you read the rest of this book get out and grab the following essentials if you can:

- Loo Roll
- Tea
- Alcohol
- Medicine
- Food

It's almost certain that the government doesn't care about you or your family at this point, so you're on your own. The up-side to this is that all bets are off, you can pretty much do what you want, but that also means bigger and nastier people are thinking the same thing. So that wonderfully free utopia you just imagined is more likely a world of constant terror.

With that in mind you should probably be thinking of survival..

SURVIVAL

In the event of Brexit the best thing anyone can do is stay at home and wait as long as possible for the whole thing to blow over. Sadly Brexit is not going to be quick.

Lead Leave campaigner and walking Victorian nightmare Jacob Rees Mogg predicted that the UK would see the benefits of Brexit some time in the next 50 years which means you're screwed unless you can hibernate or go in to stasis. Assuming that's not possible you need to learn how to survive long enough to have and raise children that can have and raise children and then finally they can have and raise children who will enjoy the benefits of what we have done.

Home defence

An Englishman's home is his castle, and you'd better make sure that your mid terrace new build is as strong as Camelot when the rabid hoards come at night with a raiding party looking for things to steal – Barricade the doors with sofas, cupboards and tables, cover the windows with planks of wood and try and make the place look like a plague infested hell hole that's already been stripped.

Under no circumstances should you let any signs of life be seen from outside, learn to live in the dark, keep noises to an absolute minimum and don't even consider a fire for warmth or cooking over if there's a chance someone will see it.

Digging an underground bunker may sound like a good idea, but you should have started doing that at least 6 months ago. A better option is to trash your main living areas and relocate your family to the loft or an outhouse. You can expect attempted burglaries at least twice a day so staying clear of target areas will conserve energy and blood.

Friend or Foe

Post Brexit it will be important to identify if people are friendly or likely to do you irreparable harm. It's a reasonable plan to simply fight anyone you come in to contact with. However there's safety in numbers as well as companionship through the grinding nightmare, shared body warmth and increased chance of hunting success. So it is best to learn how to spot who is a good guy and who is a bad guy.

If you can't see a tell tale copy of the Daily Mail about their person, then study their eyes, they are the windows of the soul after all.

Weapons

We don't all have access to automatic weaponry, so it's important to learn to throw things very hard and the best places on the body to jab a sharpened pencil. Everything is a weapon if you use it right, arm yourself at all times with whatever is at hand.

Garden sheds are a post apocalyptic treasure trove, pitchforks, shovels and rakes can keep most attackers at a distance. If you're really lucky you might even find an old chainsaw which will bump your standing up to the top of the survivalist table. Whether it works or not is almost irrelevant as the sight of it from a distance should scare off most gammon raiders.

Traps

Surrounding your home with snares, and pits will help to keep you safe as well as bringing in a steady supply of resources.

Consider using a range of sizes to protect yourself from the smallest rodent to a 4 or 5 strong gang of hungry Daily Mail readers.

Sleeping

Sleep is a double edged sword in the post Brexit world, while being asleep for as long as possible burns less calories and fights the interminable boredom, it does leave you prone to attack. If you cannot find someone to stand guard while you are unconscious, try to find a dark, secure cupboard where you can remain undisturbed for the duration.

Survival of the fittest

As society breaks down and the last tin of beans in your Brexit cupboard is emptied you'll find yourself in a kill or be killed situation. Pick your fights carefully, identify your weaker neighbours in advance. Perhaps in the early days while making friendly "This is going well isn't it?" small talk you can look out for items of value and identify flaws in their defences. Watch them, learn their routines and then when the time is right strike. Pro Brexit supporters are an ideal target, not only are they over weight, elderly and have high blood pressure, but you won't feel an ounce of guilt over your actions as they clearly brought it on themselves.

MEDICINE / HEALTH

Due to the failure of trade routes delivering fresh medicine and the loss of the electrical grid causing all refrigeration to fail, medicine will be scarce if not non existent.

While this will almost certainly result in thousands of unnecessary deaths and an increase in preventable disease, people shouldn't give up hope, instead look to the past for traditional British remedies.

Nature provides a wealth of supposed cures if you know where to look and believe hard enough, Dock leaves obviously relieve stings, Onion juices maybe cure coughs, Dandelion tea might help for arthritis, and so forth. At the very least branches can be used as a splint, fixing up a broken limb in no time at all.

New age remedies like Reiki could also be tried and simply rubbing areas that hurt, saying "there there" does wonders. Homoeopathy however should be avoided as it doesn't work at all.

Vitamins

The lack of fresh food will quickly take its toll on your body so vitamin supplements should be taken to prolong life.

As with everything else stocks of these will rapidly disappear so it is recommended that the public study basic chemistry, the periodic table and composition to understand where they can acquire minerals like Iron, Zinc, er.. Lead and the other things we need. Much of nature is made out of vitamins, so if you spot it lying around make sure you grab some.

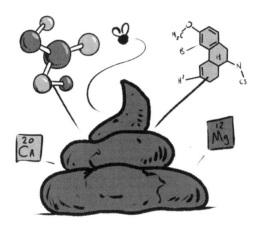

Illness

If someone is ill, keep away from them.

Disposing of a body

Grave digging will become a regular activity, so much so that you may want to consider group burials or shallow graves to save time.

Remember to strip corpses of any valuable resources and keep a note of who you have buried and where, to avoid accidentally digging them up again while excavating a new grave.

If you are unable to dig a hole due to cold weather or tiredness, then cremation offers an excellent alternative.

A burning body also provides some much needed warmth for a surprisingly long time.

FOOD

Shop shelves will be stripped bare almost as soon as we leave the EU. So get in there quick and grab everything you can, even products that would normally turn your stomach will eventually become useful on the black market or because it's a choice between a can of 'healthy option squid ink casserole' and starving to death.

Ultra long life tins and dried food are obviously the priority, but don't forget that many plastic wrapped food stuffs you would think had a short shelf life will actually last months thanks to EU advances in preservatives and packaging.

Enjoy them while you still can.

Water (and refrigeration)

The average human can only survive for 3 days without water which will be a bit of a problem when the mains pipes shut down. So start putting all of your pots, pans and bowls outside to gather as much rainwater as possible. While it is collecting start digging a large pit and filling it with your precious liquid. The deeper the pit the cooler the water will stay, which is excellent news as you've now also got a replacement for that powerless refrigerator in the kitchen. Simply place stuff you want to keep cold in to Tupperware and drop it in.

Be sure to place a cover over your pool to stop animals and passers by from falling in and drowning. It gives the water a horrible flavour.

Straining the water through an old T-shirt or sock will help remove any unpleasantness.

Rationing

Despite the Brexiteers chant of how great rationing was, it wasn't. It's a horrible exercise fraught with corruption and despair. You'll be lucky if you get any government supplied rations, as Brexit was the "Will of the people", you asked for it, even if as a Remain voter you didn't. So it's down to you to make your own sacrifices, cut back, eat less, be unhappy and you should prolong your existence.

It's impossible to calculate how long exactly this is going to go on for, so best to just start eating as little as possible as soon as possible. Your stomach will shrink so meals can get incrementally smaller and before you know it you'll be dividing individual Peas and wondering what a full plate ever looked like.

Stockpiling

Hopefully the months of fear-mongering in the tabloid press has encouraged you to turn one of your children's bedrooms in to a giant Brexit food store, rammed with extra cupboards and shelves all containing tins of vegetables and fish along with dried pasta, rice and couscous, carefully stacked like a Tetris master.

If you haven't, why didn't you heed the warnings?!

Don't panic, simply break in to someone else's house and steal their precious supplies.

To prevent the same fate befalling you, simply hide valuable items in unexpected places, under the floorboards, behind fake walls or, taking a tip from clever drug dealers, hidden away inside children's toys.

Alternatives to food

As food supplies dwindle and hunger sets in it's important to think outside the box and look for "food-like" substances to fill the gnawing hole in your stomach. Grass, leaves and twigs become a reasonably harmless buffet to tolerate.

If you have access to cooking utensils then boiling most items will reduce them to a consumable pulp. Books and magazines make an interesting "paper soup" and reading materials won't be useful in any other capacity as people lose the will to go on.

Not milk

The collapse of trade routes and refrigeration will spell the end of the dairy industry overnight, which means cows are expected to become extinct within the first few weeks of Brexit. While some patience and effort may result in a temporary solution of dog or cockroach milk, the British public will soon need to find alternatives to milk for their tea. Expensive trendy options like Soya and Coconut milk will disappear off shelves within seconds so alternative alternatives will be needed and for that you may need to use your imagination. Sometimes the appearance is all that is needed to trick our senses, watered down Tippex or diluted chalk can add a cheery milky quality to tea* or coffee**.

*boiled brown grass **diluted soil

Pet meat

While the British palette prefers cow, pig and chicken, any other animal can be a suitable alternative in post Brexit meal times.

Now is a good time to start looking at Polly, Tiddles or Rover in a different way.

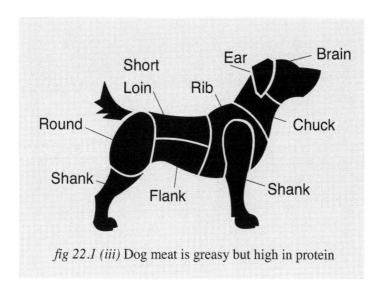

fig 22.1 (iii) Dog meat is greasy but high in protein

Jams and chutneys

Before Brexit there was great talk from the Leave campaign on how the UK would lead the way in "Innovative Jams and Chutneys". As well as providing a long lasting food source, they will become an important part of everyday life in the UK, replacing the previously world famous Automotive, Steel and Technology industries. To maintain the income lost by these collapsing businesses it is vital that every single member of the public devotes their time to Conserve/Preserve production.

Fortunately leaving the EU means that food standards and health and safety no longer apply, which means corners can be cut and production maximized.

It's not all a walk in the park though, the collapsed UK trade routes mean that you will have to source your component parts locally, stick to flavours that can be obtained during that walk in the park. Also try to be unique. The market will be saturated so try to identify flavours that no one else has thought of to guarantee customer appeal.

For example, why not try the following:

- Lego in brine chutney
- Mud jam
- Pond scum marmalade
- Quince Preserve (with a hint of cut grass and white dog dirt) Binbag jelly

WORK

Without transport or electricity the everyday commute to work will become a distant memory. But this freedom will soon lose its appeal and you will find yourself in need of employment to pass the dragging horror of existence or as a way to earn funds to purchase supplies.

Consider what skills you have, perhaps you are strong and able to clear abandoned cars from impassable highways. Or maybe you are architecturally minded and able to help construct lookout towers or resilient barricades. Then see how these abilities can be applied to the location you find yourself trapped in.

There's no point wandering from town to town looking for work, you'll waste valuable energy and the grass almost certainly won't be any greener there.

Forming a militia

It may be advisable if you find yourself existing near a group of like minded people to form a small militia. But be aware of your actions. Its easy to transform from an honest team of vigilantes clearing the neighbourhood from hooligans, into an uncontrollable raiding party going house to house enforcing your iron will on everyone and murdering those who fail to do so.

That said, forming a small dictatorship does reap considerable rewards.

Money

Due to the failure of the national grid and telecommunications systems the digital transfer of money will be non existent.

The only currency available after Brexit will be the commemorative 50 pence pieces. Each home will be awarded 10 of the celebratory coins which will be worth 12p each due to the devalued pound.

Shops

Shopping and retail work will become a thing of the past. Shopping centres will almost certainly become feral battlegrounds so best avoid those altogether unless you want to earn a few commemorative 50ps fighting in the Arndale Centre Thunder-dome or Lakeside pit of death. But trade of sorts will still be necessary and you should quickly learn the basics of a barter system, so that you can exchange your last few grains of rice for someone else's last fragments of paracetamol.

TRAVEL

It goes without saying that there will be no travel outside the UK after Brexit. While this will be cause for celebration for many who's dream Brexit was for the UK to leave the planet earth completely, it does cause problems for people with family overseas, ex-pats, businesses, exporters, ferry companies, airlines, etc. but that can't be helped, can it. Besides, the UK has sunk so low in the world's eyes that it's probably for the best.

Travel within the country will be difficult due to the blocked ports and frozen infrastructure. Motorways will become car parks within minutes and petrol supplies will run dry. Before long, people will be abandoning their cars and wandering aimlessly across the countryside.

Trains will also become economically unviable although most commuters would say they've been like that for years.

The trolley

The recommended form of post Brexit transportation will be the shopping trolley. There will be hundreds of them available at the many stripped bare supermarkets so take your pick. The trolley provides excellent stability and manoeuvrability across most terrains with all 4 wheels working independently.

The main carrying compartment is spacious enough to hold all of your worldly possessions should you need to flee an angry mob or the scene of a burglary.

It can also be used to transport the injured or dead and can be converted in to a temporary jail cell or animal trap when turned upside down.

Buses

Ironically buses (along with all other forms of public transport) will not exist post Brexit

SUPPLEMENTAL

Resources

Whether you're a nomadic traveller or a hermit encamped in an abandoned factory it's important to get the most from your resources and reduce consumption where possible.

If you find you're constantly running low on food or having to go scavenging for supplies then identify the cause of the problem and remove that.

fig 28.1 (1) An early sacrifice will help to ensure supplies last

Loo roll

Sadly the days of luxury toilet tissue will soon be a distant memory. Before society completely breaks down, remember to borrow a few sheets whenever you visit other survivors.

But once that is depleted you will need to either get your hands dirty or start using alternate materials.

Try to maximise use through multiple wipes and using both sides and remember to dry and burn the result as it is a valuable fuel source.

QUALITY OF LOO ROLL

Branded roll

Supermarket own

Newspaper

Clothing

Leaves

Dragging bum on ground

Women's "things"

Due to widespread malnutrition, Women will cease ovulating and menstruating, so sanitary products will no longer be necessary. But before you throw them out stop and consider the dozens of other practical uses.

Tampons make excellent ear plugs to protect against the constant screaming, towels placed in shoes could add some minor comfort on long walks, or stuck to the bottom of shoes to silence your footsteps when burgling houses. They also make excellent surgical swabs when stitching up battle wounds and a tampon up each nostril will help block the constant stress induced nosebleeds.

Entertainment

Hahahahahaha, there wont be any.

THE FUTURE

Your guess is as good as ours.

Why not draw what you think it will look like.

BREXIT BINGO

Tick off the events you've achieved

Barricaded your font door	Built your first man trap	Caught your first intruder	Rationed biscuits to last a week
Survived one whole week of Brexit	Had a full night's undisturbed sleep	Disposed of your first intruder	Invented a new game to pass the hours
Survived two whole weeks of Brexit	Customized your trolley	Invented a new type of idea	Had a bath
Had a hot meal	Built effigies of Leave campaign MPs	Went without alcohol for one day	Met someone who didn't try to kill you
Survived a whole month of Brexit	Ate a new type of meat	Found a secret supplyof loo roll	Escaped from an angry mob
Washed hair and shaved	Won 50p in a fight to the death	Didn't curse Johnson, Gove, May, Cameron, etc for one day	Found the will to go on

LEAVE VOTERS GUIDE TO SURVIVING BREXIT

A Gift for the Leave voter in your life

You caused this,
You fix it.

IN CONCLUSION

Farewell, good luck, and
may god have mercy
on your soul.

ABOUT THE AUTHOR

Born as a reaction to the state of the world, HappyToast wanders the internet making pithy comments about how awful everything is, while creating daft pictures and animations in a hopeless attempt at making things better.

His work has appeared across the globe, on TV and in print, he's reached hundreds of millions of people and made one or two of them chuckle along the way.

Other works by HappyToast:

- That jumping pylon gif
- Donald Trump noseflags
- Cartoon pictures of people with their willy out

This book was thrown together as an angry reaction to the UK government not producing their own guide to reassure millions of concerned citizens. It's is now 3 and a half weeks until Brexit day.

(P) Patreon.com/HappyToast

@IamHappyToast

f HappyToastArts

25973123R00029

Printed in Great Britain
by Amazon